Now and Then

Mike Blunn

Published by New Generation Publishing in 2019

First Edition

www.newgeneration-publishing.com

New Generation Publishing

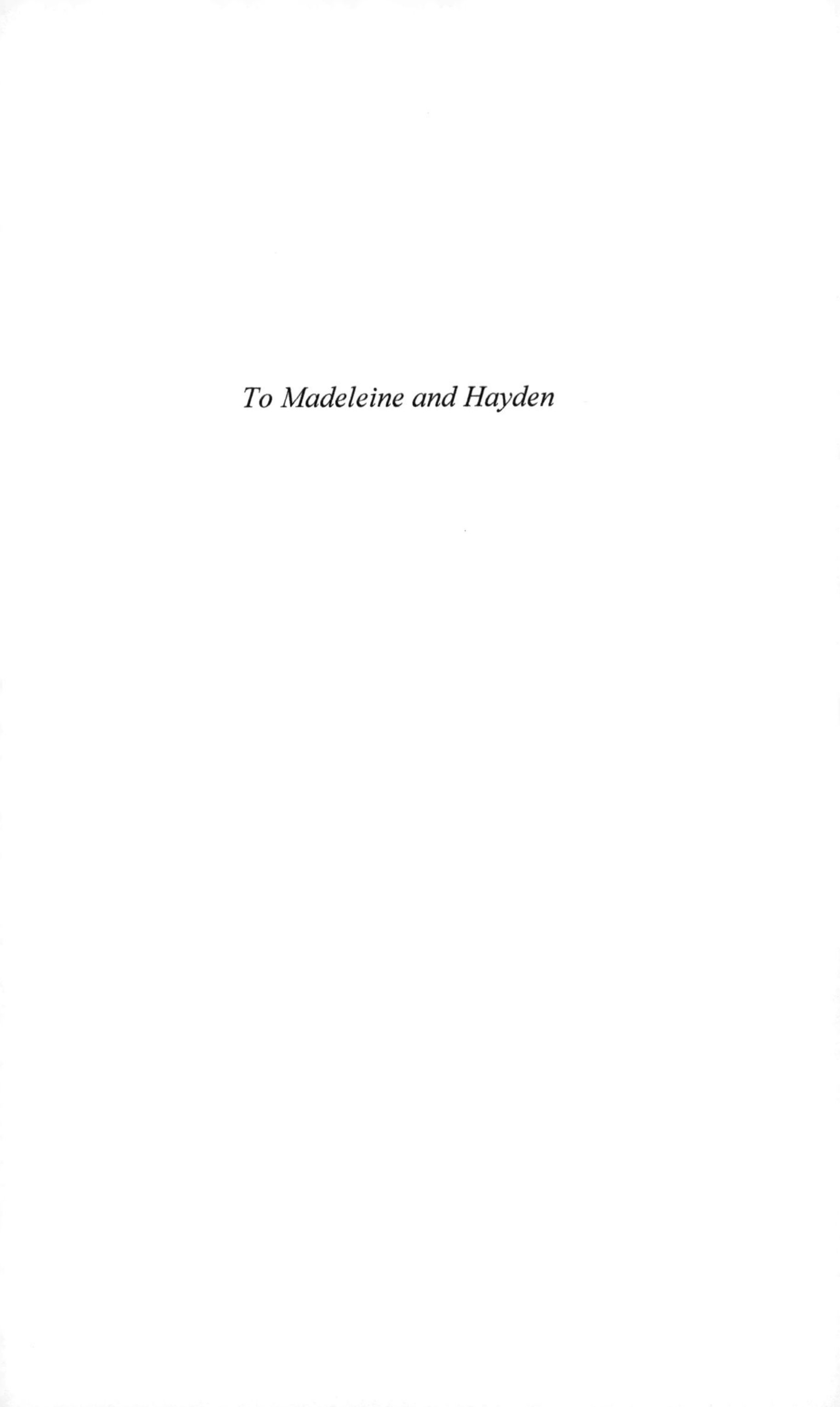

To Madeleine and Hayden

BEFORE THEN

CHAPTER ONE

1084

Paverel, or to give him his full title, Baron Paverel St. Giles de Millande, shook the spots of water from his brow and beard. He was gazing into the distance and wondering how much longer this dull, miserable weather would last. The rain had finally stopped but clouds were still drifting ominously from the west, threatening even more discomfort.

How, he mused, had fate led him to this? He was standing outside the poor farmhouse he and his companions had commandeered, waiting for some news that would show him the direction he should take on the next part of his journey.

And what a journey he had had up till now.

Paverel had been born the son of a rich nobleman way down in the south-west of France. He had enjoyed a privileged childhood with all the benefits that wealth and status could bestow. However, when he reached his early adulthood, his life and prospects changed abruptly when his father died unexpectedly. As was the custom, everything—title, lands and wealth—all went to the eldest son. In this Paverel was unfortunate in that he had three older brothers and there was no chance of any inheritance: the more so because his sharp, belligerent manner had never made him well-liked within the family. He found he had little choice: becoming a soldier of fortune seemed to be the only course for him to take.

The years following William's invasion of England had provided many opportunities for fortunes and reputations to be made. Being already a skilled swordsman, Paverel became a firm supporter to William's cause. He gathered round him a fiercely loyal band of soldiers who looked to him for example and leadership; his skill with a sword and his fearlessness in battle were outstanding. When William 11 became king, Paverel continued in his service, even becoming a Crusader, travelling across Europe to join the battle to free Jerusalem.

As the years passed, however, he began to weary of killing. When his bravery and loyalty to William earned him the title of Earl and the grant of land in the area of the forest of Berkshire, he and a few of his most trusted followers headed west. He had plans in his mind to build his own castle to rival that of his family. All he needed now was to find a suitable spot on which to build, which is why he was now awaiting news from his men. They had been sent out to survey the locality.

When his men finally returned, they brought news that they had discovered an ideal spot: a gently rising hill surrounded by forests and rich pasture land. A small but eager river flowed nearby and a useful quarry was only a short distance away. A well near the centre of the village provided water safe to drink. There was, apparently but one small problem.........

When he had digested all the news his men had brought, he determined to see the place for himself the very next day. On approaching the site the problem was obvious: the place was already occupied by a thriving village community. Paverel led his men into the village and simply ordered the villagers to leave. They were to be allowed to relocate to the outlying areas lower down the hill towards the river. In the face of group of fierce, well-armed men, some of the villagers reluctantly collected what they could carry and left as ordered. Some, however did not. Led by their elder and spiritual leader, quite a large group refused to move. Paverel drew from his cloak a rolled parchment.

"I am your Earl", he said in a commanding voice. "This decree was given to me by King William himself. It grants me all the rights over this part of the county. This hilltop is where I have chosen to build my castle, so you must all leave while you have the chance".

"Decree or not, we stay," the Elder replied. A little light seemed to drain from the sky.

"It's quite simple," growled Paverel. "You go or you die."

Being unaware of Paverel's unforgiving nature, they still declined to move.

"Kill them," he ordered. "But save that one for me," he added pointing at the priest.

A short but violent scene followed, and soon the Elder was alone to survey the carnage around him. Sixty-five bodies of men, women and even children lay strewn about him. The sky grew darker still.

"You shall always regret your evil work this day," he shouted defiantly. "I curse this place. It will always cause you pain." He paused. A full silver moon slipped from among the darkening clouds above. "Enough!" screamed Paverel as he drove his sword into the old man's frail body. The Elder shuddered and fell to the earth, staring up at his slayer.

"For your evil this day I call down ten curses on you and all your descendants for each soul murdered here today. Ten times sixty-six curses." He pointed a quivering finger to the moon. I call upon Silene above as my witness. Ten times sixty-six.....ten...times...."

With a final shake, the old man died, his dying gaze fixed on his tormentors while the moon slipped silently back behind the clouds.

"Clear this rubbish away," ordered Paverel. "Save us the best houses, but raze the rest of the village to the ground. Tomorrow we start to build."

Full night came rapidly. A column of smoke drifted lazily over the surrounding forest. The village was gone but the air grew heavy with fear.

* * * *

During the following months, Paverel organised his new life with his usual efficiency. He was, of course, required to raise taxes for the King, so he made an inventory of all aspects of his lands. Villages, fields, forests were all visited and evaluated; taxes were imposed on all of the adult population, as well as the requirement to work for one day a week in his fields. He gave each of his loyal followers an area to manage, and all the displaced families who wanted to stay were compensated with grant of a portion of land on the lower slopes of the hill leading down towards the river, or on the meadow land across the river towards the forest.

The quarry was opened up to provide building stone for Paverel's castle and for the more substantial houses. Good working men, tradesmen, builders and masons were employed and slowly a new community grew up. Work began on Paverel's castle, and a stout palisade was built to around the whole area.

Paverel married the daughter of a wealthy trader from a nearby village, and she bore him a strong son who was to grow up and continue his life's work.

All the while, however, there was a vague feeling of unease from a yet unknown source which seemed to persist.............

THEN

CHAPTER TWO

Milande Castle – Spring 1353

It had been a long and bitter winter, but spring had come quite suddenly and Milande Castle seemed to glow in the sunlight streaming from an almost cloudless sky.

In the two and a half centuries since its humble beginnings, Milande, as it was now known, had become a small but thriving town. The castle, begun by Paverel, and its tower dominated the centre, with a range of well-to-do dwellings nearby surrounding a large open area where local markets and fairs were held. Opposite the castle was a modest but quite beautiful Priory with accommodations for an order of Monks who presided over the spiritual needs of the population. Cobbled roads lead away between the grander houses to other, smaller houses where traders and artisans lived. Paverel had protected his castle and village with a strong wooden palisade with a deep ditch beyond. This had by now been replaced by a fine stone wall which circled the town. There was but one entrance, guarded by a drawbridge and strong gates which were closed from sunset to sunrise. Guards were always on duty.

The tallest building in the town was the tower attached to the castle, although it was empty and its entrances sealed. It was situated at the very highest point of the town and on the spot where the old Priest had died. It had been intended to be both a symbol of Paverel's dominance and a watch tower from which enemies might be seen approaching. Even during its construction the tower was not a lucky place. From time to time it was known to tremble as if alive. Some folk swore they heard faint but strange sounds echo round its walls. Several accidents occurred; scaffolding used by its builders mysteriously collapsed; large pieces of stone fell, and a number of workmen were killed in freak falls. One incident, in particular, caused unexpected trouble for a previous Earl. A group of the King's royal emissaries had called at the castle on the King's order. They had been given rooms in the Tower for the night. They were wakened in alarm by the quivering of their rooms and by the sounds which seemed to come from the very walls. Dressing hurriedly, they summoned the Earl, demanded fresh horses, and left quickly even though it was early morning. The Earl had then had all the entrances blocked up.

All this caused the place to be known as the Shaking Tower. Paverel had persisted with its construction however. Guards patrolled the very top. Those whose period on duty included being “top guards” counted themselves very unfortunate. Even though actual disturbances happened were not as common as supposed, all were relieved when their period of duty ended. Being assigned to the tower was often used as a punishment for minor infringements of the rules or for newer, younger guards.

* * * *

The castle itself consisted of the Great Hall and the tower. Several other adjoining buildings had been added by previous Earls. There was a large kitchen where the food for the castle was prepared; a scullery for the washing of pots and utensils, and a larder where the fresh meat and vegetables were stored and prepared. The kitchen area was more or less self-contained as it had several fireplaces where water was boiled and meat roasted. There was, therefore, a risk of fire. A brewing room provided ale which was the usual drink for most of the castle occupants, though children were given “small ale” containing varying amounts of water. Water at the castle was normally quite safe to drink as it came from upstream of the castle by way of wooden troughs and pipes. Water for everyone else came from the well on the Green, a large open space in the middle of the town where markets and fairs were held. Houses of the richer and more influential citizens surrounded The Green. Further away were the poorer houses where tradesmen and artisans lived and plied their trades.

The Earldom of Milande had passed in unbroken succession from Earl to eldest son. The present holder of the title was Earl Morgan. He had married Maria, the older of two daughters of Thomas, a prominent citizen in the neighbouring town of Anwell. Maria's younger sister, Anne, had married Richard, a dealer in cloth with a thriving business in London. They had two children, a son of thirteen, Thomas, and a daughter, Elizabeth who was eleven. Earl Morgan and Maria, however, were childless.

Morgan was a rather complicated character. By and large he was fair and just in his treatment of his subjects. He preferred to impose fines as a punishment whenever he could, though he could be harsh when the need arose. Persistent offenders and anyone committing serious crimes were branded with a cross on the right shoulder, sent away from the town, and not allowed to return. All common visitors, travellers and merchants were obliged to show their shoulder to the guards at the gates before being allowed through into the town.

If he had one weakness, it was his likeness for money. He seldom passed up the opportunity to increase his personal wealth, which was already considerable. Take, for example, his dealings with Martyn.

Martyn was a peasant farmer who worked a strip of none too fertile land. His poor plot enabled him to feed and clothe his family, but he wanted to do more than this. Though he had no formal education, he had ambition and a thoughtful mind. Each day on the way to the fields he passed the entrance to the old quarry. This had long since been worked out of all usable building stone and lay derelict. Martyn had approached the Earl through Peter, the Earl's bailiff, and had agreed to rent it on a yearly basis for two pennies a week to be paid in advance. He had had to borrow some money from his father to make the first years rent. Each year in March he would bring the rent for the next year. His plan for the quarry was innovative but risky. There were a few serfs who made a poor living by catching fish from the river and selling them at the weekly market. Fish was quite a popular meal when it could be bought but there was never enough of it. Martyn's plan was to cut a narrow channel from the river and to flood part of the quarry. He used discarded pieces of stone to enclose a small section, making a shallow pond. He planted reeds and irises from the river around the margins. In the breeding season he bought several large fish and allowed them to breed in his pond, removing them afterward as they might eat the young. For the next two years he made more ponds, stocking them as he went along. At the end of the third year some of the fish in his first pond were big enough to sell at the weekly market. They proved popular, and he soon began to show a profit on his investment. His venture, however, was not unobserved. Morgan had been well informed of the trade in fish, he could see more money to be made for himself and told Peter of his plan.

When Martyn met with Peter to pay for his next year's rent, he had a shock.

"The quarry is no longer for rent," said Peter. "The Earl has other plans for it."

"But what about me? What will happen to me?" he asked.

"The Earl is offering you a position as a fish warden. You get every tenth fish for yourself. That is, in my opinion, a generous offer:--and, of course, you will not have rent to pay!"

*　　*　　*　　*

One of the most recognisable inhabitants of the town was Limpy. This was not, of course, his given name. No-one actually knew what it was; he probably didn't remember it himself. As a young child from one of the poorest families, he had deformed legs caused by rickets.

Because of this condition, he had been slow to avoid a loaded wagon when playing near his house, and his foot had been crushed. For the rest of his life he had been unable to farm. All normal occupations were denied him and he became a sort of recluse, pitied by many and avoided by some.

He nevertheless had a secret smile on his face this evening as he limped home from the Town Inn. The owner had allowed him to become a helper at the tavern. He collected pots at the end of each evening and cleared the floor once a week, putting down clean reeds or straw. No-one guessed why he had volunteered to take on such a menial task. He was paid but two pence a week and yet he seemed satisfied. He had a secret. When clearing the floor each Saturday night, he paid special attention to one part of the room-the part where the better-off wagered money on a variety of gambling games. As the revellers gambled they drank large quantities of strong ale. Often, during the course of their gaming, coins, usually pennies, would be dropped and would become buried in the thresh on the floor. While carrying out his cleaning, these would find their way into Limpy's pocket. The reason he was smiling to himself this night was that he had found a groat, which was worth four pence, more than twice his weekly wage.

Another citizen more used to the shadows than the light was Ranwick……..

CHAPTER THREE

The early morning sun had touched the top if the tower: the guards were opening the town gates. Market Day. Families from outlying homesteads crowded in. Farmers, eager to secure a favourable spot on the Green poured in carrying their produce or driving carts poured in. Twice a week stalls each costing 1d. a day would be set up and a wide range of food, provisions and artefacts were displayed for sale.

Bread, eggs, cheese and varieties of meats crowded among displays of leather goods, steel implements and roll of cloth.

An ox lumbered in dragging a cart laden with hay forged forward, all but colliding with a tall bent figure in a worn brown cloak with a hood pulled over his head. Ranwick muttered a curse, but paid little heed to the chaos going on around him. As the only apothecary he was both revered and feared. A person had to be quite ill to seek his help, even though his advice was usually sound.

Ranwick had a somewhat chequered past. Intelligent though a little headstrong, he had studied medicine at Oxford University, supported by moderately wealthy parents. The demise of his father brought his studies to a premature end and he went wandering across Europe, doing a variety of work to survive. He learned of many local cures and about the power of plants to aid healing. In 1342 he had returned to England, eventually finding himself in Milande. He had rented a small dark room beside the Shaking Tower because it was cheap. Even though in a prime position, no-one cared to live in such a place.

Ranwick didn't seem to mind. The place was filled with a collection of pots, jars, flasks and mysterious boxes filled with dubious assortment of powders, chemicals, seeds and bones. Great bunches of flowers and herbs hung in disarray from the rafters, dropping petals and leaves on the floor below. Sweet and pungent smells mingled to fill the room. This alone was sufficient to deter all but the bravest of clients.

This morning, however, he was on the move. Clutching a small bag containing a few popular herbs and remedies to his chest, he followed one of Morgan's guards through the rain to the Great Hall. The Earl had demanded his attendance. He was a little concerned to find that all guards and servants had been dismissed, and that he was confronted by only Morgan and Maria.

"Well", Morgan began, "have you good news for me regarding our little problem?"

"I'm afraid not, my Lord."

"None at all?"

"I'm sorry, my Lord, that I can find no answer to your difficulty beyond what I told you before. You will have no heir because your wife is unable to bear children."

"Is there, then, nothing to be done?"

"Nothing I would dare to suggest to you, my Lord."

"Then you are of no use to me," shouted the Earl. "Go, and think yourself fortunate to still be in one piece."

Ranwick turned and scuttled from the room, feeling that keeping low for a while might be the best course of action to take.

CHAPTER FOUR

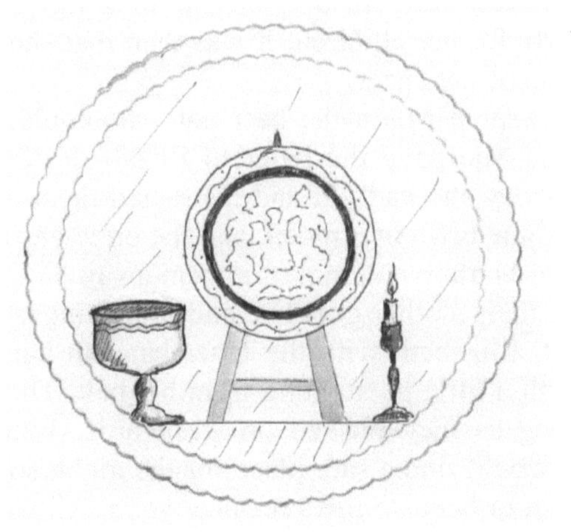

LONDON

Summer 1354

By contrast, Richard and Ann, Maria's younger sister, had raised a young family. There was Elizabeth, a pleasant girl of thirteen, and Thomas, a cheerful, noisy boy of eleven. Richard had been a cloth merchant with a thriving shop in a fashionable area of London when, some years earlier the Plague had struck him down. Somehow the rest of the family had survived, but Elizabeth was no businesswoman. She had been cheated by former clients and suppliers until there was barely a business left. In despair, she took ill and could not care properly for her children. It was then that she decided to seek the help of her sister.

Having written Maria the best note she could, she called her children. She gave the letter to Elizabeth, together with the little money she had left and instructed them to find their way, first to the town of Anwell, and the on to castle Milande. She felt sure Maria would not turn them away.

Bidding their mother goodbye and promising to return, the two set out; Elizabeth with the letter beneath her dress, and Thomas with a little purse hung from his belt. The days were hot and long as they pushed on westwards. When evening came they would find a safe place for the night, sometimes in a disused hut or beneath the trees in a wood. All went well for a while, and then danger came. Tom, who was leading at the time, called for Elizabeth to keep up.

"We still have a long way to go, come on!"

Getting no reply, he turned only to find his sister in the grip of a pair of robbers armed with wicked-looking knife. The pair demanded that they give them their money.

"But we have none," cried the girl, trying all she could to break free.

"Who would travel across the country without money?" the smaller one asked. "Now, your purse or the girl dies".

Reluctantly Thomas handed it over. "No", shouted Elizabeth, "that's all the money we have in the world."

"It will be alright", said her brother, "we'll manage somehow."

The thief grabbed the little bag and tipped out three pennies into his grubby hand. "It's not much", he grumbled. "You had better get on your way. Quickly now, before I change my mind". The children ran off as quickly as they could, Elizabeth well in the lead.

"Come on, slowcoach", she called, and Thomas slowly caught her up.

When they were well away for the evil pair, he sat down on the grass and took off a shoe. "What are you doing now?" she demanded. Thomas did not reply, but instead removed a cloth lining to reveal the rest of Mother's money carefully hidden away. He took out three more pennies and placed them carefully in his purse, tying it to his belt once more. "That was a clever trick," said his sister in admiration.

"We may need to do it again before we get to Milande," said Thomas.

The two made slow but steady progress over the next three days, sleeping at night in old huts or under hedges. They used some of their money to buy bread in villages that they passed. By the end of the fifth day of their journey they emerged from a wood to see, a short way off, a modest town built on a hill and surrounded by a stone wall. Light was fading fast, and though they were very tired, they hurried as fast as they could uphill towards the large wooden gates…….

* * * *

Lemuel was the person in charge of the day to day running of the Great Hall. He welcomed visitors, arranged their accommodation and saw to their needs. He oversaw the servants, making sure that they all fulfilled their duties and that nothing was overlooked. As a much younger man, he had been chosen to travel as body servant to Morgan to France in the service of King Henry. There, he found food and lodgings, cleaned his armour and tended to the horses. When Morgan returned to England after the battle to defend Calais, Lemuel was given his present position, which he found greatly to his liking. He had a way of dealing with other servants. Any indiscretion, however minor, was treated very seriously with severe punishments threatened. At the last minute, however he would seem to soften. The relief felt would engender a deep feeling of gratitude towards Lemuel and ensure complete loyalty. This would result in him being informed of any unusual activity within the castle. If this news was important, of course he would inform Morgan, but other items he kept to himself. Although he could not read or write, he had an amazing memory. Nothing was forgotten. He had another unusual ability. Although a large man, he had the knack of walking very softly. He would sometimes appear almost magically in a room and witness actions or overhear conversations without anyone knowing. He learned many things this way, and kept them for future reference. It was through him that Morgan first learned of the night's visitors.........

Late the previous evening, long after the castle gates had been closed, the guard on duty became aware of a timid but persistent knocking.

On peering through a small grille in the Judas gate, by the light of a flickering torch he could just make out two small grimy faces.

"Please, please let us in," the larger figure pleaded.

"Go away," replied the guard. "The castle is closed for the night. Come back tomorrow."

"But we have travelled a long, long way and have nowhere to go", cried the smaller one.

"Go away, I say," shouted the guard.

"We have brought a message for a lady called Maria," cried the other one.

The guard hesitated. Then he sent for the Captain of the Guard: let him make the decision. The captain listened to the guard's story, and peered through the grille himself. The visitors seemed to be alone and harmless, but, on the other hand, rules were rules. What to do? In the end, he took pity on them.

"Let them in," he ordered, "but take great care." The gate was opened a little, and the two children squeezed through. "Put them into the guard room, and be sure to watch them carefully. I will decide what to do next in the morning."

It was a worried and thoughtful Captain who made his way to the Great Hall to give his report. He had decided not to mention the incident of the previous evening, not being at all sure his action would be met with approval. He was taken completely by surprise, therefore, when the Earl asked, "And how are our guests this morning?"

The Captain stood bemused. How had the Earl come to know about the children so quickly? In the corner of his eye he glimpsed Lemuel melt silently into the background. So that was it. But how did Lemuel find out? It must have been one among his guards…… he would see to that later, if he survived. He was used to the Earl's ways, having worked in the castle for so many years: he knew lying was not the way forward.

"They seem well enough," he said. "They were extremely tired. They were given food and allowed to sleep in the guardhouse and were still asleep when I looked in this morning."

"There is a rule, is there not, that the gates are to remain closed during the dark hours?"

"That is so, My Lord."

"Then why were the rules, *my rules,* not obeyed?"

The captain hesitated. His career, and maybe his life, depended on his answer.

"It was not an easy decision," he began, "but I asked myself, "What would the Earl would do if he were here at this moment? Would he deny two small, vulnerable children sanctuary for the night?" I felt sure you would want them to be safe. Is that not so, my Lord?" Morgan could see that he was in a corner. He could not do anything but admit the Captain's action was fair.

"Quite so, Captain. As this was an exceptional case, I will accept your explanation. But, in future, be sure to get authority from me before breaking any more rules."

"Of course, my Lord," said the Captain with a sigh of relief.

"Go now, and when they wake, see that they are brought here to me."

"Yes, Lord." He bowed and quickly withdrew. That had been close!

* * * *

In his absence the gates had been opened, and, as it was a Market Day, the whole place was alive with noise and laughter. Pushing through the throng he reached the guard post. The children were awake, and were recalling their adventures to the spellbound guards. He saw to it that they looked as presentable as possible, under the circumstances, then led them out through the crowds to the Great Hall. There they had to wait a while until the Earl had dealt with the morning's business. At last they were admitted to find the Earl and also his wife waiting for them.

"These are our new guests," said Morgan. He pointed to the girl.

"What are your names?"

"If you please, Sire, my name is Elizabeth, and this my brother, Thomas."

"And how old are you?"

"I am thirteen and Thomas is eleven."

"Nearly twelve," added the boy.

"You have travelled far?"

"Yes, Sire. We have come from London where we lived."

"I have relations in London, in Stepney," put in Maria.

"And tell me. Why have you come?"

"Our mother and father kept a shop until father was killed by the plague some years ago. We tried to help Mother in the shop but it was too much for us. Last year Mother became ill.

She gave up and took to her bed and could not look after us. She gave us what little money she had left, and sent us here."

"But why here?"

"She told us to find someone called Maria, and that perhaps she would take care of us."

"And exactly who is this "Maria"?" asked Morgan.

"We do not know for sure Sire, she did not say, though I think she may have been a relative of mother's," Thomas put in, keen to be part of the conversation. "Mother said she was pretty, kind and would be sure to help us if she could."

"She gave us a letter to give her, if we found her," said Elizabeth. "Please, is there anyone in Milande of that name"?

"Tell me. What was your mother's name?" asked Morgan.

"She was called Ann. We always remember it because she was born in Anwell. We used to say that the town was named after her."

"Enough," said Morgan. "You must be in need of a rest. Go with this servant who will take you to the kitchen for food and a drink. Come back when we send for you."

They followed down stairs, along dark corridors and through to a large busy room where they were fed and allowed to rest. Meanwhile the Earl and his wife were in earnest discussion. Could it be that their mother was actually Ann, Maria's younger sister?

"We must question them further," said Morgan. "Have them brought to us again."

When led back into the Great Hall again, they began to feel a little more at ease.

"There are some more things we would know," began Maria, "mainly about your family. First of all, what was your father's name?"

"He was called Richard. He bought and sold cloth, some of it from abroad, Italy and France in particular. He sold some of it in the shop, and mother used some to make fine dresses to sell," said Elizabeth. "I was learning to be a needlewoman when mother became ill, but I could not work quickly enough to keep the business going."

"And do you, perhaps, remember your grandparents?"

"No, my Lady. I never actually met them. My father was an orphan who was brought up by an aunt, but we were named after my mother's parents Thomas and Elizabeth. When they married, they left home to start up their business in London."

"And do you have any other family that you know of?"

"I once overheard my parents speak of a sister, but that is all I know," said Elizabeth. "And Thomas was too young to know anything at all."

"There is one more thing I must ask," said Maria. "It may seem strange, but tell me, did your mother care about animals?"

"Yes, she did," said Elizabeth.

"All except dogs," added Thomas. "She really didn't like dogs. But I do."

Maria turned to her husband. "Then it must be as we thought! Ann hated dogs from the time wild dogs attacked the horse she was riding. The horse reared up and she was thrown to the ground. She wasn't badly hurt, but she always had a fear of dogs afterwards."

"Please, my Lady, do you know of anyone called Maria? You see, I have a letter to give her. My mother gave it to me as we left and said I was to keep it safe until we found her."

"And where is this letter?" asked the Earl.

"I have it here, if it please your lordship" Elizabeth replied.

"Then I think you had better show it to us. There is a person I know called Maria. It would seem that your letter may be meant for her."

Elizabeth reached into the folds of her dress and produced a piece of very fine cloth. She handed it to the Earl.

"We must decide what to do," said the Earl. "Meanwhile, Lemuel will see that you are looked after. Tomorrow we will have some arrangements made for your future."

The children left the Great Hall respectfully and spent much of the rest of the day exploring the market and the streets around the Green. They slept once more in the guard room and awaited what life had in store.

The Earl carefully unfolded the cloth. On it, in a shaky hand was a plea for her children to be given care and protection. It was marked "with respect, from Tiny to Red."

"That is proof indeed", said Maria. "I would call her "Tiny" as she was so much smaller than I, and she called me "Red" because of my red hair. Who else would have known that?"

Morgan and his wife considered the matter at some length. In the end, they decided that the children should be allowed to stay in Milande, but that they should be give some suitable employment. They would live in the servant's quarters for the time being. Elizabeth would become a maid to Maria and continue with her needlework. Thomas was no quite so straightforward, however. He would have to become an apprentice to a craftsman: this would be an unpaid position until he gained basic skills. There were a number of possibilities. At last, it was decided that he would become a silversmith.

* * * *

CHAPTER FIVE

Fendrel hummed quietly to himself as he opened the shutters of his shop ready for the day ahead.

Fendrel lived in a small house on a side street well away from the Green. He lived on the ground floor, as did most folk in the area, but he had a small working area raised up and reached by a rickety ladder. Here he could carry out his delicate cutting and engraving without the distraction of passers-by. There was one small opening in the south wall, which allowed the brightest of the daylight in. In the evenings and on dark days he worked by the light of candles. For the most detailed work, he allowed himself the luxury of a beeswax candle. This was expensive, but it gave a steady, brighter light than the tallow candles normally used.

Today, however, the sky was clear, promising a good light for the delicate piece he was working on at present. He was engraving a fine pattern on a large silver plate for the church altar. Commissions for the Prior did not come along all that often but when they did they were quite lucrative. The Prior was head of the Monks of Milande Priory. Though not a large Church in number, nevertheless it was quite a rich one. The Earl had his own private Chapel, but he would sometimes attend the morning worship. Such occasions ensured a full church: all were anxious to be seen, and it was well-known that absences were noted.

This new plate would be used to collect donation made at the end of the service. The sheet of silver had been cut and slowly and carefully beaten into shape. Today he would begin chasing the fine pattern around the edge. It was the part of the work he enjoyed most: here he could fully express himself in the curves and scrolls which linked together to form the complicated decoration around the edges and rim.

Now that he had been persuaded to take on an apprentice he could leave him with the basic, mundane work of cleaning and polishing the bowl he had recently finished.

Thomas was in the living area. The work was not complicated, though it demanded concentration and dedication, neither of which Thomas possessed to any degree. He soon found his attention wandering. Though not a main thoroughfare, the street had a steady number of passers-by. There was always a steady stream of people, carts and horses making their way past the open doorway. Folk would peer inside and pass the time of day. Thomas would often be drawn away from his polishing to chat, and the day would slip away before he knew.

"Hello Thomas," called a little voice. Looking up he saw Jenet's smiling face peering from the doorway. Jenet lived outside the gates in the village down by the river. "Are you coming to the fair tomorrow?"

"I shall be working as usual, I expect. Market day is just like other days for me."

"But tomorrow is more than that. It is the feast of Saint Andrew, and there will be lots of things to do and see. Everyone has the day free."

"Fendrel hasn't said anything. I must ask him when he comes down for his morning break."

"Perhaps I shall see you, then. I will look for you, but I must go now or I shall be late and get into trouble!" Jenet slipped away to do her errands.

Later that evening Thomas and Elizabeth discuss the coming Holy Day. This would be their first since leaving home, and the weather promised to be good. It was all very exciting.

The next day, indeed, proved to be sunny and warm: just the weather for a fair. In the morning there was the Parade. The Prior and the monks led the way from their cloisters carrying the richly embroidered banner of St. Andrew and the great Golden Cross. As they went, they chanted, and the following crowd of townspeople and villagers followed along. Through the streets they went, gathering more and yet more folk following behind. They paused at the Great Hall for Earl Morgan and Maria to join in at the head of the procession. On they went into the cool shade of the Church for the Service of Praise. At the end of the prayers, all streamed out onto the Green.

"Look, there's Jenet," Thomas shouted as he pulled his sister along.

The three of them wandered excitedly between the rows of gaily decorated stalls. Elizabeth had brought with her the last of the money given to them by their mother. They paused a while to think of her, and wonder how she was. "There must be some way to get news from London," said Elizabeth. "Perhaps I could ask Maria what we might do."

"Come over here called Jenet. There are some acrobats!" They watched in amazement at the way they jumped and turned cartwheels. "I wish I could do that," said Thomas.

"I expect you could learn," said Jenet. "I'm sure you could!"

One ran sprang into the air, turning right over and landing on his feet. How the crowd cheered and applauded!

Moving on, they watched a juggler tossing large knives into the air and catching them as they fell back to the ground. Amazingly, he went through his act without even a scratch!

It was, however, the egg swallower who caused the most fun. Standing in front of a gaily coloured tent stood a small, stocky man dressed in a long sleeved tunic which reached almost to the ground. While the audience waited silently, he solemnly selected an egg from a small basket before him. Standing sideways to the crowd, he slowly raised the egg high, opened his mouth wide and carefully lowered the egg to let it slide down his throat: or so it seemed. The egg actually dropped down his wide sleeve, but the illusion was convincing. The crowd clapped, but Thomas could not believe his eyes. He pushed forward eagerly to ask how the feat was done, and as he did, he brushed against the performer's coat. A cracking sound, a gasp form the crowd, and an eggy mess dripped onto the ground. The audience howled with laughter, thinking it was all part of the act. Embarrassed, Thomas was dragged away and was soon swallowed up in the throng.

Thoughtful Elizabeth had brought with her a halfpenny from what little remained of the money her mother had provided. With it they were able to buy them each a piece of gingerbread as a treat. When they had been all around the Fair, Jenet thought it was time for her to go home.

"Would you both like to come to my house on Sunday," she asked. "I could show you round the village, and you could meet my brothers."

This proved to be a popular idea.

"Of course we will, and thank you," said Elizabeth.

* * * *

"What do you mean? What is the problem here?" Morgan was not in the best of moods.

Lemuel shuffled his feet. "Fendrel the silversmith has an issue with the young Thomas, my Lord."

"What is wrong? I thought that things were arranged."

"They were, my Lord, but Fendrel says he cannot keep Thomas any longer. Normally, he would by now be progressing from Apprentice to Journeyman. This means he would need to pay Thomas a small wage from now on. He feels, however, that although he is a fine boy in so many ways, he is not cut out to be a silversmith, even though it is an enviable trade. Fendrel says that he cannot concentrate long enough at a time: he is too easily distracted. His mind is very active, and he would flourish at a more physical occupation."

"And what do you suggest?"

"I wonder if he would be better suited at, perhaps, blacksmithing. He would find it more of a challenge, my Lord."

"Very well, just see to it. I need to see the boy gainfully employed. Do what you will. I leave the matter in your hands. I have more important things to attend to. Just keep an eye on him."

"Yes, my Lord." Lemuel withdrew, grateful that what might have been a difficult time had not been as uncomfortable as it could have been. Finding a suitable place, however was not to prove easy. The work at the smithy was too heavy. At the stables, the horses were too large for

Thomas to handle, and he spoilt a whole day's ale by not paying enough attention when he was give his instructions. Finding him work was not going well.

* * * *

While Thomas's future seemed uncertain, Elizabeth proved to be quite an asset. She had learned the basics of being a lady's maid: how to help Maria dress; arranging the various costumes and seeing to the washing and pressing her expensive dresses. It was, however, her skills as a needlewoman which made her reputation at Milande. She had brought with her from London a few precious tools. There was a thimble. While many thimbles were made out of strong leather, they tended to be rather cumbersome. Elizabeth's, however was made of brass with dimples punched covering the outer surface. She also had an ornate pin case and a pair of scissors made of iron. Her prized items, however were her needles. Most needles were made of bone, but hers were of bronze, allowing the finest stitches to be made.

Isabel was Maria's Chief Dresser. She was an elderly but valued servant who had long been in charge of Maria's wardrobe. She was kind enough towards Elizabeth. Her sight was slowly fading, though, and she envied the neatness of Elizabeth's work and began to see her as a sort of challenger to her position; she made sure she received all the credit and praise from Maria.

CHAPTER SIX

The following Sunday, after the church service, the children eagerly made their way through the great gateway and down the broad path to the river. They had arranged to meet Jenet near the bridge, and they were pleased to see her waiting for them. This was actually the first time they had seen the village in daylight: it had been dark on the evening they had arrived. Spread across the slopes between the castle and the river were a great assortment of houses, mostly single story with shelters and animal pens nearby. This part of Milande had been developed by the original villagers expelled by Paverel many years ago. Many of the peasants were farmers, each working a portion of land on the far side of the river. A good part of the land belonged to the Earl, and was worked for him by the inhabitants of the village in return for a piece of land which was just about enough to support a family. In a good year, there was enough for the family and a little extra to sell at the market. When the busy times such as ploughing sowing and harvest came, all had to work first on the Earl's land even if it meant neglecting their own plot.

There were other workers, though, apart from the farmers. There were the builders and carpenters who built and repaired the houses in the town. There was always work for skilled men. New houses were needed for the steadily growing population; repairs and renovations to the castle and the church provided continuous employment; pews for the rich and benches for the rest, though many preferred to stand near the pillars where there was usually a better view.

"Come, now. Come and meet my family," said Jenet and she led the way through the straggling paths to a small but cared-for house with a pen of chickens nearby Jenet lived with her father, mother and four brothers. The older two worked in the field with father, and Jenet helped by looking after the younger ones and doing the housework. On market days she would be sent to the town to buy the things they couldn't get nearby. Elizabeth and Thomas were made welcome by the family, and they learned much about village life. Elizabeth told the about their earlier life in London, about how they had lived over their shop in Stepney and the death of their father. She told them of being sent away when mother became too ill to care for them.

"So we ended up here in Milande,"she said." The Earl has given us the chance of a new life here. But I wish we knew how mother is. She must feel so alone, though the neighbours are very kind." She grew silent for a moment or two as she remembered what her life had been like.

"Come and see the rest of the village," said Jenet. They said "Goodbye" to the family and followed Jenet down to the river. Near the bridge was a small house. "That's where the bridgeman lives," said Jenet. "All merchants and visitors have to pay a toll to cross, but not the villagers. The bridgeman collects the money and takes it to the castle each week. The money pays for repairs. Last year it was damaged in a storm which weakened the supports. Boatmen ferried people across, but their small boats could not manage animals or carts, and the market was closed for several weeks. Some folk held a temporary market over there in that field." She pointed to a grassy area between the river bank and the forest.

"We didn't pay to cross," said Thomas.

"There's no traffic when it gets dark, so the bridgeman goes home," said Jenet.

Thomas leaned over the bridge and stared at the water below. "There's a river near our old home," he said. "It's not very clean, like yours, but it is much, much bigger. It is so big that boats and big ships can sail along it."

"I know what a boat is, but what exactly is a ship?" asked Jenet.

"Oh, Ships are very big boats. So big that men cannot row them. They have strong tall poles called masts on them which hold up big sails made of thick cloth. When the wind blows, the sails catch the wind and the ship moves forward."

"So the ship has to go the way the wind is blowing," said Jenet.

"Mostly, yes", agreed Thomas, "but sailors – the men who work the ship – use ropes and things to turn the sails so that the ship can move to the right or left as well."

"They must be sight to see; but where do they go to?"

"They sail down the river and out across the sea to other countries, carrying goods and things. I sometimes went to watch them being loaded or unloaded. It's very busy and noisy. Carts come along bringing things and people to the ships."

"I wish I could see them," said Jenet. "You know so much more than I do."

"But it is so much nicer here'" said Elizabeth. "It is so quiet and peaceful. You have all these fields and trees and so much green, green grass. London is so crowded, grey and noisy."

"And it smells," added Thomas.

He turned to look at the far river bank. Beyond the grassy meadow were the forest trees. A thin plume of smoke drifted way in the distance.

"Is the forest burning?" asked Elizabeth.

"Oh no," laughed Jenet, "that is probably old Peter. He builds fires to make charcoal. Then he sells it. George the blacksmith uses a lot of it. When he has enough, he loads up his cart and takes it to sell in the town".

Thomas turned to look downstream where a large building hunched over the edge of the river bank.

"What's that, and why is it so close to the water"?

"That's the mill, where the miller lives. He grinds the corn we grow into flour. Then we can make our bread to eat".

"How does he do it? Can we go and see"?

"Yes, of course. But not today. Like most folk, the miller does not work on Sundays. Perhaps you could come again soon".

The two waved goodbye, and climbed the path to the town gates. They were reminded of the first time they had come here, and they gave a wave to the friendly Captain who had kindly let them in, almost at the expense of his own position. As they approached the castle, however, something seem to be different. Not many folk were about, and those who were seemed anxious to be elsewhere. "What is the matter?" they asked of one passer-by. They woman did not look up, but shuffled one past murmuring only "Best get yourselves home, and quickly", and hurried off.

Back in the warm safety of the castle kitchen, they asked one of the cooks why folk were disturbed today. She told them that from time to time the tower became "alive", shaking as if might fall. No-one knew when it might happen, but it was linked to an ancient curse place upon the place many years ago. The doorways to the tower had long since been sealed off, and no-one went near at these times.

The following day Lemuel came for Thomas and told him that the Earl was annoyed that no position had been found suitable for him. He was to be given one last chance.

"You are to work for Ranwick", Lemuel said. "And if this fails, you will go out to the village to work as a peasant farmer". He took Thomas to the room next to the tower where Ranwick lived, and banged on the door. After a while, they heard a key turn in the lock, and the door creaked open slowly. Thomas was ushered inside and down several steps. He turned back to Lemuel only to find that he had already scurried away. He turned back to the room, the like of which he had never seen before. Candles supplemented the meagre light coming from high windows. As his eyes became accustomed to the dim light, he saw that almost every available space was filled with a wild assortment of boxes and pots. Heaps of things lay strewn all around. He was startled when one of the larger piles moved.

"So you are to be my new companion, are you?" the pile said, thus revealing it to be, in fact, Ranwick himself.

"I am told so, Sire," Thomas replied without much enthusiasm.

"Very well. There are certain basic duties for which you will be responsible. You are to look after yourself entirely: I have not time to waste on you. You will see that there is water always available: you will trim the candles and replace them as necessary: you must empty the night-bucket, tend to the fire and answer the door to visitors. There will be errands to run from time to time, but above all, do not move anything. There is food over there. We will share whatever there is. You may have questions to ask, but only when I am not busy. Do you understand?"

"Yes, sire," he replied. Thomas was already sure he would not like it here, but he knew he had no other choice; working in the fields in all weathers did not appeal to him one little bit. At least it was shelter and fairly warm. That was strange. Although a small fire burned in the far corner, it hardly seemed enough to keep the cold at bay in such a large room.

By the end of the week he had more or less settled in. He saw to his duties, but without enthusiasm.

CHAPTER SEVEN

It is Sunday. Ranwick's custom is to attend morning service in order to keep up his standing as a prominent citizen. Thomas is to attend also, though he does so reluctantly. They join the others waiting for the arrival of the Earl and his retinue. Thomas was very surprised to see that at the end of the line, neatly dressed, was the figure of Elizabeth. Maria had made her one of her companions. Thomas suddenly felt proud of his sister. She had obviously been making the most of her chance while he himself had not. He decided there and then he would work hard to do the same.

Over the following weeks and months he became a different person. He listened carefully to Ranwick when he explained what he was doing, and made himself more than useful, doing all his tasks with a new enthusiasm. He followed Ranwick on his occasional trips to the meadows and woods to collect the roots and herbs he used in his potions. He learned their names and the best places to find them. He carried them carefully, hanging them to dry as he had seen Ranwick do. His questions and comments became more pertinent and he began to be trusted with the simpler daily tasks and he began enjoying his life again. All the while certain things puzzled him. One was the room itself. Although there was a fire which kept burning, he was sure it was not sufficient on its own. One day he mentioned this to Ranwick, who motioned for him to stand on a stool near the wall at the side of the room, lean over the benches and table and touch the wall. To his surprise the wall was not cold as he had expected, but somewhat warm to the touch. Ranwick told him that this wall was actually part of the tower which was the centre of general concern.

"There is, I believe, no danger here. I have observed carefully over many years and am sure we are quite safe. One day I may tell you more........"

There was another thing which Thomas had observed but could not understand. From time to time Ranwick seemed to disappear. He had put this down to his imagination but intended to watch more carefully in future. Then one day his chance came. One moment Ranwick was busy and the next he had gone. Thomas was certain the door had not been opened; indeed it was locked and the key was there in the lock still. Slowly and quietly he set about searching the room. It was quite large with any number of corners to hide in, but though he took his time, it was clear that Ranwick was gone. Completely mystified, he took up station near the door to see when Ranwick should come back. He could not quite believe, clever as he was, his master had the power to become invisible at will. He was quite astounded, therefore, a few minute later to find Ranwick moving about the room as if nothing had happened. Somehow he could not pluck up the courage to say anything this time but he resolved to see if should happen again. It did. Not often, but from time to time. Thomas was almost convinced that he served a man who could disappear at will. It was but a few weeks later that his mystery was solved.

Thomas decided he could not keep quiet any longer. He simply had to know what lay behind Ranwick's disappearances. He chose a day when things had gone well and Ranwick was in a talkative mood.

"Please, Ranwick, there is something I need to ask," he began.

"Well, what is it?"

"I don't know quite how to put this," said Thomas, "but, well, sometimes, well, you sort of disappear. Have you by chance, some magic which makes you invisible? There have been times when I simply can't find you."

For a few moments Ranwick stared at Thomas with his piercing eyes, as if he was unsure just how to answer. At last he made up his mind. Thomas was to be trusted. He drew nearer and began to explain.

"No, I have no magic. But before I go on you must swear never to tell anyone what you are about to hear."

"Yes, Ranwick, I swear."

Again he hesitated. "If I could only be certain. What I am about to say could be dangerous for both of us. You must never speak of it to anyone but me. Are you sure you want to know?"

Thomas now saw a different side of his master: he obviously wanted to talk, but he was still not absolutely sure. "Yes, I want to know, and I'll not speak to anyone, I promise."

"Very well, so be it. Come, I must first show you something."

He led the way across the room to the far side. There he hesitated again, then finally he pulled a heavy looking table aside. On the wall there hung an old tapestry decorated with strange signs. Ranwick carefully pulled this aside and Thomas was surprised to see a small, stout door. It opened easily with a large key which hung from a cord hidden beneath Ranwick's cloak. He took up a candle and beckoned Thomas to follow.

"Come, then."

Together they passed into a large circular room. It was dank and musty.

There was but one small window too high up for Thomas to see out. It was guarded by an iron grille and let in only a feeble light. As his eyes became used to the gloom he could see evidence that the place had been used as a sort of storeroom. There were blocks of stone and wooden beams pushed to one side: the accumulation of many years.

"What is this place?" he asked.

"You are now inside the shaking tower. But there is no need to be afraid. All is quiet today."

"But everyone says that the tower is sealed because it is dangerous, and no one can get in!"

"We can! You see, when I moved into my room I found the doorway blocked up. I was curious, so I gradually opened it up. It took a good many weeks. I wanted no one to guess what I was doing so I worked quietly in the evenings when I could be sure of not being seen."

"But you must have been afraid when the tower shook."

"The first time, yes I was, but over time I found nothing to harm me, so I carried on. So now you know. Let us return and I will tell you the rest of the story."

They left the tower room, carefully closing the door and replacing the tapestry and pushing the table back in place. Thomas found some bread and cheese for supper and the two settled down near the fire.

"Why does the tower shake so? What does it all mean?" asked Thomas.

"That is what I have set out to discover," explained Ranwick. "I have learned some things, but not everything. I know that in the folk legend, many of the people from the old village died to protect their homes. The ground was cursed ten times for each of the sixty six people slain, and that Silene, the moon goddess was called upon to act as witness. I know when the tower will shake, and have tried to find out what happens inside that room."

"But no-one knows when the tower will shake," said Thomas. "It comes on different days and at different times."

"I know", replied Ranwick.

"So when you go into that room, you are working."

"Yes, and it is not easy moving that table on my own, especially since you have been here. But now you know my secret, you could be of great help, if you wish to."

"You have been good to me, and I like it here. I will do whatever you may ask."

"Have a care," warned Ranwick. "You should never promise to do anything until you understand what it is you are promising, and what it may mean to you. But now it is late. We will talk again, and I will tell you what I know"

* * * *

One morning the Earl called for Elizabeth to attend him. She was a little nervous, still. She had a good relationship with Maria who had always treated her kindly. But Earl Morgan was another matter. She entered the Great Hall and waited respectfully while matters of important business were conducted. At last she was called forward. Today he did not seem quite as imposing as usual.

"I'm sorry," he began. Then he hesitated. "My messengers arrived from London last evening." Again he paused. "It would seem that your mother is dead, my child. She never recovered from her illness. The shop was sold to pay her debts, and there is nothing left for you in Stepney. You should now consider this to be you only home. And your brother's, of course. How are things with him now?"

On reflection, Elizabeth realised that their mother had understood her position, and had sent them away to spare them. All the same she could not help the tears slowly filling her eyes and running down her pale cheeks.

"Thomas enjoys the things he is doing, Sire," she replied. "He has learned much and is great help to Ranwick. If you please, might I go now and tell him about Mother?"

"Yes, of course. Go quickly, and be of what comfort you can to him." She curtsied to the Earl, then made her way out into the town and across the Green. She had a strong dislike of the tower and she shivered as she knocked on the door to Ranwick's room. Thomas himself answered the door and signalled for her to follow him.

"Please, Ranwick, this is Elizabeth, my sister."

"Come in, child. Thomas has spoken of you many times. What brings you here?"

Elizabeth told them her news and hugged Thomas tightly.

* * * *

It was some days later that Ranwick returned to the subject of the tower. Thomas had reminded him several times of his promise to tell him more. One evening Ranwick asked if he had thought more about discovering the tower's secret.

"Yes, I would like to help. What can I do?"

"It could be dangerous, I just don't know," he began. "But this is what I have learnt. One day, when I knew it was time, I placed a small cage containing two mice in the room to see what they would do."

"And what happened?"

"Nothing, as far as I could see. They were still there and seemed to be unaffected, although they had hidden themselves under the straw. It was quite some time before they ventured out again. The next time, I put a stray dog in there. It, too, was unharmed, but it was rushing round and round, behaving oddly. It was clearly frightened. So again I had learned nothing apart from the fact that no physical harm had come to either the mice or the dog. I began to feel I would never know the tower's secret. Then, the next time things got even stranger. I got the bird catcher to find me a large bird. He came one day and brought me a crow he had trapped. It was a fine bird. When the next episode was due, I left it in the room." He paused.

"Well, do go on – what happened to the bird?"

"I don't know," said Ranwick. "I really don't. Because, you see, when I entered the room next day, the bird was not there. It had vanished! I search everywhere, but it was nowhere to be seen. As you saw, there is only the one door, and only you and I know of it. There is, of course the one small window, but that is covered by those iron bars. There is no room for a bird that size to get through. Only maybe a mouse might escape that way; certainly not a fully grown crow! I searched everywhere, but not even a feather remained! I <u>must</u> find out what happens there. That is where you can help, if you are brave enough."

"What is it you want me to do?"

"Would you be willing to spend a day in the tower? I cannot do it myself as I would be missed if folk come for herbs or potions. And there is a heavy table to move. I am sure no harm will come to you. But if you would rather not I shall understand."

Thomas was silent for a while. At last he looked up and said "Very well. I'll do it!"

"Only if you are sure."

"Yes, I am," said Thomas. "But you haven't said how it is you know when the shaking comes."

"Many times I have seen that the shaking comes only when the moon is in the sky, and when it is at its largest: a complete moon."

"That cannot be so," said Thomas. "The moon shines at night, but often the tower shakes in the daytime!"

"That's because sometimes it can be seen in the day, if you know when, and can look carefully. The next large moon will come the day after tomorrow, so that will give us time to prepare – if you are brave enough."

"I'm ready," said Thomas. "Just tell me what I have to do!"

* * * *

Inns are places notorious for news and gossip. After a tankard or two of ale, tongues become loose, and, in a spirit of competition, tales true and not so true are repeated and frequently embellished upon. Anyone so choosing might glean many a story by simply sitting and listening. By the very nature of his employment Limpy heard many things. Most he discarded as meaningless, but occasionally he came across snippets of information which potentially might be of use.

These he stored away in his mind, for although somewhat physically challenged, he had a retentive memory. He was often able to put to good use the results of his eavesdropping. Today it was a villager whose comments caught his attention.

Nathaniel was a chandler of sorts. Mainly he collected unusable scraps of meat from around the village, more especially from the butcher. He had a hut and a shed well away from the rest of the other villagers where he would render the scraps down to collect the greasy tallow. Using dried rush stems he would fashion simple tallow candles which he would sell. When lit these would give out a pale, mellow light. They were not very bright and they produced plenty of smoke, but they were cheap enough to be afforded but most of the village.

It was, however, the mention of a “special” candle that attracted Limpy’s attention. Ranwick, of all people, had asked for a “special” candle. These were made not of tallow, but of the wax produced in their hives by bees. Most of the wax candles were made by the monks, who kept bees. Part of the honey produced was made into mead which they kept for themselves. The wax was then used to make candles for the church and the Earl. Wax candles burned slowly and more brightly than tallow ones. The produced little smoke and gave off a pleasant, sweet smell. They were also costly; far beyond the means of most ordinary folk. So Nathaniel being asked for a wax candle was quite unusual. What did Ranwick want it for? Limpy wondered.

Nathaniel bought the sticky wax from the local keepers of bees. He heated water over his fire and stirred in the wax. The honey dissolved in the water, and this sweetened water he would sell on later. The wax melted and rose to the surface. After allowing the liquid to cool he removed it. He used it to make his “special” candle by melting it and pouring it down a wick made from twisted threads. This required time and patience. After allowing it to cool a little, he carefully rolled and shaped it to the required size. All this meant that the candle was costly, and just what Ranwick wanted with it was a mystery Limpy would do his best to solve.

* * * *

It was Friday morning. Ranwick and Thomas continued to make their preparations for the weekend.

“Since we will be busy on Sunday, it might be as well if you let Elizabeth know you will not be seeing her at the Church as usual. Perhaps we should let it be known that we may be taking a trip at the weekend. She could become worried unless she knows where you are. We can’t have her coming round here to see you.”

“Where shall I say we are going?”

"We could be going to Anwell to collect some special herbs. That would account for being away Saturday and Sunday. You must be in the tower on Saturday evening. By the way, this is for you."

He carefully unrolled a piece of coarse cloth to reveal a thick yellow candle. "This will last the whole day, so you will at least be able to see fairly well, whatever happens."

"I've only ever seen such candles on the altar in church. How did you get it?"

"Don't worry; most things can be got if you know who to ask."

And so the work went on. Thomas managed to see Elizabeth in the afternoon. She accepted the news of the trip without question. "Just be careful – you know the sort of people you may meet, especially in the forest."

"We'll be alright. Most folk fear Ranwick and do all they can to avoid him if they can."

Saturday evening saw Thomas installed in the tower room. They had assembled a sort of table from discarded stones and wooden beams opposite the small grill-covered window. The candle was placed there well away from any breeze that might disturb its steady glow. Thomas settled down on a heap of straw next to the table, as if the stones might offer him some protection should he need it. Now that the time had come he no longer felt as brave as before. However the thought of solving the centuries-old puzzle kept him going. Ranwick, too, was showing uncharacteristic nervousness. He fussed about, ensuring there was nothing more that Thomas might need. At last, he declared that it was time for him to close the door.

"Try to remember everything you see and hear, Thomas, but whatever, I will be back in the evening of tomorrow. Now try to get to sleep; the large moon will come early tomorrow. Then, who knows….. Oh, and one last thing before I leave. I want you to have this." He took a small purse from beneath his tunic and handed it to Thomas. When he opened it he found a small, shiny gold coin. He had never seen such a thing before, let alone held one.

“What is it?” he asked.”

“It is a noble,” said Ranwick. “There will be another one for you tomorrow”.

“Thank you, Ranwick” said Thomas as he tied the purse safely to his belt.

Ranwick left the room, carefully closing the stout door behind him. Thomas heard the heavy curtain being drawn across, and the bench being dragged into its place. There was no way out now; he was sealed in. Now his mind began playing its tricks. What if Ranwick did <u>not</u> come back? What if something happened to him? What really happened so many times in this lonely room? Well, he would soon know one way or another. He tried to push bad thoughts from his mind and as Ranwick had suggested, he tried to sleep. It was not easy. He was cold, even with the blanket he had, but in the end he fell into a troubled, fitful sleep.

* * * *

It was late on Saturday afternoon, and getting dark. Limpy’s mind was not on his job. He had got no further with his problem over Ranwick. All he had heard was a rumour that Ranwick and the boy were away somewhere, but no-one knew where or why, or even cared. No-one, it seemed, had the slightest interest in what the apothecary did or didn’t do. He lurched awkwardly between the long trestle tables. Some complained when he knocked into them, but he didn’t seem to notice. He just had to do something. On impulse, he slipped out of the inn door. It was quite dark by now as he crept from shadow to shadow towards the tower and Ranwick’s room. Despite repeated knocking, the door remained obstinately shut. There was one small window high up-too high for Limpy to reach but he knew it was covered on the inside anyway so there was nothing to see. He almost shouted out in sheer frustration, but not wishing to cause attention to himself, he held back his cry and reluctantly turned towards the inn. It was then that his weak leg gave way as it often did. He staggered forward, crashing into the obstinate door.

After a brief moment's rest, he slowly levered himself to a sitting position. As he did so, he caught a faint glimmer of light which squeezed its way between the wall and the doorframe. Light? But Ranwick was away, *wasn't he?* He pressed close to the wall but could see nothing. This added to his frustration and further fuelled his determination to find out just what was going on. Leaning he back against the door, he eased himself upright and slowly he made his way back to the inn.

When Thomas woke, he sensed that he was not alone. As he peered round the room the feeling grew steadily. The silence he had enjoyed so far was disturbed by faint whispers. No, not whispers, but rather voices far away. Many voices: voices raised in protest: voices calling out, but still some way off, afraid. Shadows appeared and moved about him. The noise got louder and more insistent. The room was soon filled with ghostly figures swirling around and calling, shouting.

Though bewildered he tried to record in his mind everything he saw. Sometimes the cries formed words. He heard shouts of "NO!!" and "Have mercy" mingled with the sounds of the sound of fighting which grew louder and louder until he became deafened and crouched against the wall while the battle raged round him. Then, after one piercing shriek, the room became silent once more. Even so, it was some time before Thomas relaxed enough to look around. He could see that the room had changed. His table and candle were gone, as was his bed and the food he had saved from the previous evening. The walls were intact but the floor was strewn with stone and more beams and a thick dust covered everything. The window. There was something different there, too. It took a while before he realised what it was. The grill! The iron grill which had been so firmly set into the stone wall was gone. As the light grew stronger he began to explore. The iron bars, now almost rusted away, lay in the debris on the floor. The room was still not silent. faint sounds coming from outside caught his attention. He had to look outside. He struggled to form a pile of loose stones to form a rough platform. Gingerly he climbed up and peered out. If the room had changed, then so had the view, although he could not see a great deal. Trees still dominated much of the middle ground, with fields and hedges away in the distance. From here he could see little of the ground nearer the tower. He remembered he had promised Ranwick he would learn as much as possible, but there was little more to see from here. Now that the bars were gone there might be enough room for him to squeeze through: but was he brave enough? He might simply tell Ranwick that he had seen nothing (which was true) but there was still the matter of his own curiosity, which at last, overcame everything. He climbed down to the floor and searched until he had some pieces of stone which were fairly flat but not too hard for him to handle. Climbing back onto the platform he found he was high enough now to work his shoulders through the gap in the wall. Looking down, he now saw that the ground outside was now very far below him. After taking one last look around the room, he raised himself up and dropped lightly to the grass below. Cautiously he looked around. The first thing he saw was that the mill, the bridge and the whole village and villagers were gone. The whole area was completely overgrown. Bushes, brambles and stunted trees had replaced everything. He decided to work his way round the walls of the town. This took far less time than he thought. There was no town. All that remained was the tower and a few crumbling parts of the wall. Where the town had been lay a large number of grass and weed-covered mounds. Thomas could hardly believe what he was seeing. He was alone. Almost. He had spotted a solitary figure which had emerged from the trees below and begun to climb the hill. From time to time the figure disappeared among the bushes, but it slowly advanced towards the tower. Thomas watched for a while as the man, (apparently it was a man), got nearer. Thomas decided it might be best if he were not seen. He chose a particularly bushy area and crouched down to wait.

NOW

CHAPTER EIGHT

Anwell 2013

It was Thursday afternoon and Jack was having one of those weeks. Everything seemed to be crowding in on him. The office of Hughes and Pendle (Solicitors) where he worked was in turmoil. Several important letters had gone missing, half the staff were down with a mystery bug and the annual audit was fast approaching. He was really looking forward to the weekend. He piled his papers into his briefcase and set off for home. Throwing his things onto the back seat, he climbed into the little pink Fiat which he and Penny shared. It hardly seemed like the sort of car he would like to drive, but money was tight after the move and with all the expenses of setting up their new home, but today he was grateful for the illusion of sanctuary which came with the closing of the door.

Home for Jack and Penny was a "starter home", (two bedrooms, a garage and a very small garden), in a new development on the edge of town. The centre of the town of Anwell was old, with narrow streets and quaint houses which seemed to lean against each other for support. In recent years, however, the town had grown outward considerably. For the time being, then, they had an open view over surrounding countryside. He parked the car and let himself in. He allowed himself a short rest, then set to work preparing their evening meal as on Thursdays Penny worked late. She sometimes wondered whether it was worth it, as Jack used almost every pot, pan and utensil in the tiny kitchen. Clearing up took forever.......

When she arrived home, Penny wore a worried look.

"I had a phone call today", she said, "from Mum's friend and neighbour, Mrs. James. She told me that Mum wasn't too well though of course she didn't want to make a fuss. Perhaps I should go and see her at the weekend".

"Of course you must go", said Jack. His mother-in-law had been very kind in giving them a home while they saved for their own place. She lived a fair distance away in Bristol.

"There is so much work on at the office at the moment, but I will come with you if you would like me to."

"No, I'll be fine. I'll leave early on Saturday morning and you will have some peace and quiet to get on. I should be back late on Sunday. Will you be alright fending for yourself?

"I'm sure I'll be o.k." he replied. "Anyway, there is always the pub!

Friday came and went. Penny packed a small bag ready for the morning. When Jack woke, he found that his wife he already left. The motorway traffic would build up during the day, and she was anxious to find out how her mother was.

Jack prepared a simple breakfast then settled down to his work. It was helpful that the morning was dry but rather grey and dull. It was, in fact, late afternoon when he finally decided to call it a day. He rose stiffly from the table and collected his papers together. He had not stopped for lunch and was feeling hungry. He would treat himself to a quiet mead out. Collecting his jacket he headed for the door, stopping only to pick up his wallet and a walking guide which he stuffed into his pocket.

The Coachhouse was quiet when he walked into the small Snug Bar. He ordered a meal and a pint of beer then retreated to a window seat. While he waited, he drew the booklet from his pocket and found the right page. His road, being new was not yet marked, but he soon found the pub and the neighbouring farm. He let his eyes roam over the map and made up his mind that, weather permitting, he would venture out into the countryside. But where? Then a small cross caught his eye. The word "Ruins" made him wonder, and he decided to make that his destination. There was a small track marked past the farm and out across several fields. It didn't seem too arduous a walk, so, to the ruins he would go.

The next day, Sunday, seemed a bit brighter and the forecast even suggested sunny periods later. Jack ate a modest breakfast, then found his back pack and loaded it with a few essentials. In went a waterproof coat, his map and compass, a notebook and pencil. He checked he had some cash in his pocket. He would not be needing his wallet. He prepared a couple of sandwiches for lunch, together with some biscuits, chocolate, an apple, a banana and a bottle of water.

He left the house, locked the door and headed off down the road. He turned off down a wide track which led to the farm. The track slowly became narrower and more overgrown. He leant on a gatepost and consulted the map. He checked his compass, and decided he was heading in the right direction; several more fields to cross, and then he should come to a wood. Time to get on. The clouds had begun to thin a little, and a gentle breeze urged him on. Twenty minutes later he stopped again. He had reached the edge of the wood. He had hardly noticed, but his path had been rising steadily and he needed to get his breath back. Idly he looked around less sure of his way, now. Then he saw it. Barely upright, almost crouching among the brambles, was a rickety wooden signpost. It was so old he could only make out a few odd letters. "--STL-"was just visible. From this he guessed it had once read "Castle", but the rest was illegible. Taking another look at the map, his way seemed to be straight ahead through the trees. There was just a faint path, probably made by animals as not many walkers came this way.

Not being one to give up easily, he lifted his pack again and plunged in among the trees. The undulating track lead where ancient trees jostled with saplings for a share of the sunlight which filtered from above. It was just about clear enough to follow, until he came to a place where the track forked. Here he hesitated. Left or right? From the bearing he took he chose the right, uphill path. He became a little less sure a while later when his way dipped downwards towards a more open, grassy area. There, a small river meandered from right to left. True, it was not particularly wide, but the ground on either side was less than firm. Still not wanting to give up, he explored his side of the river in both directions. A fallen tree, bent over the water seemed to offer a solution. He was still undecided what to do when he noticed that on the far side, the trees were thinning and the ground rising once more. Onward! He gingerly climbed onto the fallen trunk and inched his way out over the water. His efforts were rewarded when he clambered down on the other side. The ground rose gently and the trees gave way to an extensive area of bushes and brambles. At the top of the rise, still some distance away, he saw the object of his trip. He climbed on up through the shrubby growth and hilly mounds. The main feature was a round tower which stood at the very top with the remains of its supporting walls. The stonework seemed sound enough when he clambered around. The tower itself was in good condition, though it had an almost forbidding air. Jack tried to visualise what it must have looked like. As if to crown his achievement, the sun finally broke through and the clouds melted away bathing the area in warm sunshine. Checking his watch, he found he had been walking for almost two hours, so he decided to rest a while. Choosing an inviting corner he settled down to enjoy the peace and quiet. Idly his eyes roamed over the tower. It was circular, with two small windows, one at the top and the other much closer to the ground. He would have to find out more about this place; how old was it? Who built it? How many generations had lived here? What had become of them? Perhaps he should start with the local library.

A small movement behind a nearby bush caught his attention and he was taken with the strange feeling that he was being watched. Perhaps it was his imagination. He decided to ignore his watcher, and reached for his haversack and removed his lunch: sandwiches, fruit and his drink. He selected a sandwich and began to eat, all the while keeping watch on the bush before him. Again there was a slight movement; a small figure; a boy, perhaps.

"I see you," he called. "Come on out of there."

Nothing, then another vague movement.

"Come on, there's nothing to be afraid of. I shan't hurt you."

He waited again.

This time the figure rose slowly and peered at Jack through the leaves. Ever so slowly a small shape stepped from the cover of the bush. Jack was right, it was a small boy, but quite a strange one: not what he had been expecting at all. It was the way the boy was dressed that was disturbing. He wore a rough tunic, caught up in folds at the waist and tied with a sort of cord. His shoes, if that is what they were, had flat soles tied at the ankles with the same kind of cord. The boy's eyes were bright but wary. He kept watch on Jack as he slowly crept forward. His glance flicked from side to side as he took in this strange person, his bag and his lunch – especially the lunch. Jack noticed this and slowly picked up a sandwich and held it out.

"You look hungry," he said, "come and have something to eat. I have plenty." The boy's looked hard at the food, but he kept his distance. At last he began, haltingly, to speak.

"What are you? Where are you from? What strange fine clothes you wear. You must be rich."

Jack's feeling of unease returned, but he offered the sandwich again. This time the boy darted quickly forward, took it, and retreated again. He took a long cautious look at it, then took a small bite. Jack pretended to ignore him and went on with his lunch. The boy decided that the food was good, if rather strange, and wolfed down the rest.

"Would you like some more?" Jack asked.

"I have not had such bread before. It is very good."

"Come and sit, then. There is plenty for two."

The boy came slowly forward and crouched down, out of arm's reach. Jack watched in amusement as the boy quickly ate two more rolls.

"What's your name and where do you live?"

"My name is Thomas, and I live here," the boy said, waving towards the ruined stones, "but everything is changed. Everyone has gone."

A small tear welled in the corner of his eye.

"Ranwick, Elizabeth and even the Earl. They have all gone."

"Well, Thomas, I must say that I am a bit puzzled. You say you live here. But not in these ruins, surely?"

"There were no ruins when I was shut in the tower. There was a big town filled with houses and people."

Jack could make no sense of what he was hearing, but the boy spoke earnestly enough. Jack went a bit further.

"Who shut you in the tower, then and why?"

"Why Ranwick, of course. Only he and I know of all this."

"So why did he do such a thing? Was it some sort of punishment?"

"No. Ranwick wanted to find out what happened when the tower shakes. I was to try to see what happens. When the shaking stopped, I climbed out of a small gap in the wall to have a look round. I expect that it what happened to the crow. It never came back, you see. And now all the town is gone." He turned to Jack with tears running down his face. "Please, shall I ever see my sister again?"

Jack couldn't think of a suitable reply to this so he paused to offer something more from his lunch.

"Here. There is an apple or a banana. Which would you like? You can choose!"

"I know an apple, but I've never seen the other thing before."

"It's a banana – try it, if as you say you've never had one."

Thomas took the fruit and slowly took a bite. His face wrinkled in disgust.

"It is <u>not</u> good. I don't like it!"

Jack smiled. "You have to take the skin off first!" He reached into his pocket, produced his penknife, cut off the end of the banana and peeled back the skin. This time Thomas took only a very small bite, then ate the rest quickly.

"I can't believe you haven't had one before, Thomas. Everyone knows what a banana is."

"I don't."

"How about oranges or pineapples? Have you heard of them?"

"No."

Jack was now thoroughly confused. The boy seemed so open and honest. There was a ring of truth about everything he said, but how could he not know about such ordinary things. He couldn't be lying, or could he? No, there was no reason why he should. Though he could scarcely admit it, he felt inclined to believe him. He would try again. He dug into his haversack again and found two small chocolate bars. He gave one to Thomas.

"Here," he said, "have some chocolate. You must know what chocolate is."

"No, what is it?"

"You eat it of course. But take the wrapper off first!"

He ate a little and found he liked it.

"You have many strange things. Where do you live – you are not from Milande."

"I live way over there beyond those woods in a town called Anwell."

Thomas jumped.

"I've been to Anwell,"he said. "My father and mother lived there before they went to London."

Jack was now thoroughly confused. How could he have been to Anwell? Had he really live in London? He turned. Thomas was staring intently at the fields beyond the wood.

"What is it?"

"There, across those fields. I can see bright things moving."

Following the boy's gaze, Jack could just make out the sun glinting off the windows of cars passing along the by-pass.

"Those are cars. On the main road."

"Carts? They can't move that fast!"

"Not carts, cars. You do know what a car is, surely?"

"No, I've not see one of those."

Jack was out of his depth. Just who was this strange lad who said he lived in a ruined town? Did he really not know of ordinary things such as cars or oranges or had he some sort of memory problem? He needed to find out more. Reaching into his pocket, he drew out a lighter and handful of loose change.

"What are these?" he asked.

Thomas stared for a while, and then said “Those must be coins, though they are very fine. You must be rich.”

“I’m not! But look.” He picked out a shiny two pound piece. “Whose picture is this?”

“I don’t know. Ranwick has been teaching me to read and I see some letters there. That looks like my sister’s name. She is called Elizabeth”.

“It is. Elizabeth is the Queen, and that is her picture.”

“What is that?” Thomas asked pointing to the lighter.

“It’s something to start fires with,” said Jack, not wanting to become involved with explaining all about cigarettes. “You just press here like this and then you can light a fire from it.” Thomas drew back a little and stared at the bright little flame which magically appeared near Jack’s thumb

A weird thought passed through Jack’s mind. Mentally he began to put some strange facts together. He had been to Anwell and had lived in London, yet did not know what cars were. His clothing was rough and old, but thought Jack had unusual clothing. He recognised money but not Jack’s coins. And surely he had seen a lighter before! How could this be? He was jolted from these thoughts by a loud cry. Thomas pointed wildly at the sky, then ran back and hid again behind the bushes. Jack looked up to see a plane in the distance slipping slowly earthwards, probably heading for Luton.

“It’s only a plane,” said Jack. “It won’t hurt you!”

“I don’t like it here,” he said coming out from behind the bush. “It’s not the same. Everything has changed.” He stopped suddenly. “I must go. I hope Ranwick will be waiting. The Moonday is nearly over.”

“What do you mean, “Moonday”?”

“It is when the moon shines big in the sky. Ranwick can tell when it will be. I must go. Here, this is for you.” He pressed something into Jack’s hand and then with one last look at the remains of the picnic he turned and was off back to the tower. Jack rose and followed him just in time to watch the boy lower himself through a small window he had not noticed before. He was at a loss to know what to do. Kneeling down, he called into the darkness "Here, take this" and he dropped in the second chocolate bar. He could see nothing in the darkness. He wished he had a torch. Thomas' voice filtered faintly.

"Thank you. I will come again, if I can, the next time the moon is grown. Will you be here?" He heard a pleading in the voice.

"I will. Promise." Suddenly he realised what it would look like for a grown man to be talking to a wall. It was as well there was no one. He got to his feet. There was nothing to do but to repack his haversack. Only then did he realise that his penknife was missing; so to was his loose change and the lighter. With a last glance at the strange tower he retraced his steps down to the river and through the wood then across the fields to the lane. All the way he relived the events of that strange afternoon, his mind wrestling with conflicting ideas. He had a lot of thinking to do. He was about to see if a pint of beer would help when he remembered that his money was gone, so he continued on through the estate towards home. Then another thought struck him. What would he tell Penny? She was sure to ask where he had been. He could not lie, but what would she make of his odd tale. She would find it hard to believe. In the end, as he opened the door, he decided to say as little as possible. In the end he would tell he everything. But not now, later.

It was when he was emptying out his bag that he found it. Lying down at the very bottom was a shiny coin. That was what Thomas had put into his hand. He took it out and studied it. It seemed to be gold. The inscription, however made him stop and stare.

* * * *

Thomas crouched down in the darkness, wondering what was going to happen next. He did not have to wait too long. He shrank into the corner while, once again, the room seemed to spin, and the air was filled with unearthly voices. After what seemed an age, the room became quiet once more. Another wait in the darkness, and then, at last, he heard the sound of the secret door being opened. Suddenly, Ranwick was there at his side. He was so relieved that he could hardly speak. Gently Ranwick reached out and helped him up before leading him back out into his familiar room. All the time he thought about which of his little treasures he should show him.

I wonder.......

If you were Jack, what would you tell Penny about the strange boy you met at the castle?

What do you think she might say and do?

If you were Thomas, what might you tell Ranwick about the Traveller you met?

Would he believe you?

Would you show him all the things you had brought with you or would you keep something secret? Why?

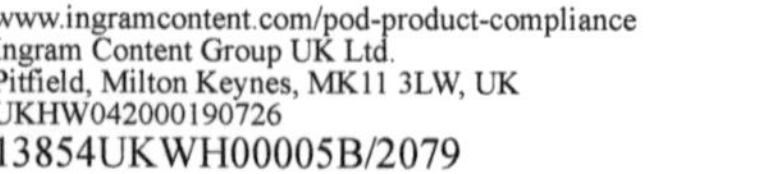
www.ingramcontent.com/pod-product-compliance
Ingram Content Group UK Ltd.
Pitfield, Milton Keynes, MK11 3LW, UK
UKHW042000190726
13854UKWH00005B/2079

9 781789 554953